For Karen Lotz
and my friends Across the Pond
at Walker Books
M. M.

To a queen and her princess,
Donna Gath Criswell
and Sharon Marie Gath
P. H. R.

MEGAN McDONALD

illustrated by Peter H. Reynolds

JUDY MOODY

AND THE

RIGHT

ROYAL

TEA

PARTY

WALKER
BOOKS

official stuff

First published 2018 by Walker Books Ltd
87 Vauxhall Walk, London SE11 5HJ

This edition published 2019

4 6 8 10 9 7 5 3

Text © 2018 Megan McDonald
Illustrations © 2018, 2010 Peter H. Reynolds
Judy Moody font © 2003 Peter H. Reynolds

The right of Megan McDonald and Peter H. Reynolds to be identified as
author and illustrator respectively of this work has been asserted by them
in accordance with the Copyright, Designs and Patents Act 1988

Judy Moody ™. Judy Moody is a registered trademark
of Candlewick Press Inc., Somerville MA

This book has been typeset in Stone Informal

Printed and bound in Great Britain by CPI Group (UK) Ltd

British Library Cataloguing in Publication Data:
a catalogue record for this book
is available from the British Library

ISBN 978-1-4063-9235-7

www.walker.co.uk

MIX
Paper from
responsible sources
FSC® C171272

JUDY MOODY

AND THE
RIGHT ROYAL TEA PARTY

Table of Contents

Her Royal Highness,
Judy Mudeye Moody

King Richard the Moody

Queen Kate the Great

Sir Short Shanks

Who's Who

Jessica Finch

Royal Secret Keeper

Mudeye

Thirteen Times Great-Grandpa

Grandma Lou

Royal Moody Sapphire Bearer

Lady Philberta Finch

Keeper of the Royal Songbirds

Fit for a Queen

Judy Moody had been Doctor Judy, M.D. She had been Judy Monarch Moody and Madame *M-for-Moody*. She had been a Girl Detective and a Mood Martian. She had even gotten a picture of her famous elbow in the newspaper.

But she, Judy Moody, had never been a queen. Not even a Queen Bee of Spelling. Not even Queen for a Day at the Pamper-Me-Royal Nails and Spa like Mum and

Grandma Lou. She had never slept in a queen-size bed or sat on a Queen Anne chair. She had never eaten an English queen cake or laid eyes on a queen ant.

In fact, her eight-year-old life had been very UN-queenly so far.

Until now!

Judy was making a tree for social studies. Not a tree with leaves. Not a tree with acorns. A *family* tree! A tree with grandmas and grandpas and aunts and uncles and cousins.

Grandma Lou came to help. She brought lots of old pictures and papers. She had charts and calendars and lists with names and dates in old-timey handwriting.

"What is all this stuff?" Judy asked.

"Your Grandpa Jack traced the Moody family all the way back to your thirteen-times great-grandfather. Did you know you're related to a Moody who was on the *Titanic*?"

Judy sat up. "You mean that giant ship that sank? I saw it in Stink's *Big Head Book of Disasters*."

"That's the one. When the ship hit an iceberg, the young Mr Moody helped people into lifeboats 12, 14, and 16 before he died."

"Whoa," said Judy.

"And if you go even further back on the Moody side to the time of Queen

Elizabeth I, you have a British cousin. The name Moody means *brave*, and this fellow was known for his bravery. The story goes that he rescued a prisoner from the Tower of London."

"Tower of London?" Judy asked. "You mean the castle where they keep all the jewels?"

"Yes, but they used it as a prison, too."

"So my cousin rescued someone from the Tower of London?" Judy couldn't believe her ears. "Maybe he rescued a princess! What if he was a prince? That means he was related to the queen. So my cousin was a royal!"

Judy fell right off her chair. This was

news. BIG FAT news. She had royal blood. She, Judy Moody, was just-might-maybe related to a queen!

RARE!

Wait till she told Tori! Tori was Judy's pen pal from London. As in England! As in where the queen herself lived! Tori knew everything about the Queen of England. She had probably been to tea at the queen's house.

Palace, that is.

Speaking of tea, Grandma Lou went to put the kettle on. Judy had to write to her pen pal right this very second. She ran upstairs and grabbed her Grouchy pencil.

Dear Tori,

LSS. Long Story Short: I just found out
I am related to the queen! Maybe now I will
get to come across the pond and ride that
London Eye ferris wheel after all. What can
you see from up there? Big Ben? London Bridge?
Buckingham Palace – the queen's house? I bet you
can see the whole entire city, including the royal undies
drying on a clothesline behind the palace. Ha, ha.

WBS and tell me queen stuff!
Thanks!

PPF. Pen Pals Forever,
Judy Moody

Me ↓

Judy pinched herself. She didn't feel
any different. Same old Judy.

Maybe if she put on something purple?

Queens wore purple. Judy loved all things purple. She had a purple sock monkey, a purple mood ring and a purple skipping rope.

One whole wall of her room was painted Saltwater Taffy purple. "Purple is the colour of royalty, Mouse," Judy told her cat. *Kings and queens and princes, oh my!*

Judy plumped a purple pillow. "Here, sit on this, Mouse. You're a royal cat now. Just think – being related to a queen is like … if *you* were related to a lioness."

Mouse dove under the rug. "Mouse, I dub thee Royal Mouse Catcher."

Judy snatched her fuzzy purple bath-robe from behind the door. She draped it over her shoulders like a cape. Her royal robe! Every queen needed a streak of purple hair. She sprayed a hunk of hair zombie-purple with purple hair spray.

Brill-short-for-Brilliant!

Judy dug in the back of the closet for an old cardboard crown from Royal House of Pizza. A few stick-on jewels would jazz it right up. She slipped on her candy necklace – just like priceless pearls. *Chomp!* She ate a purple one.

Judy Moody took out her Famous Women Rulers ruler. Cleopatra. Amina. Lili'uokalani. Queens, queens and more queens. Not just princesses. Queens of Egypt. Empresses of China. Queens of England. Maybe even queens related to her great-great-great-great-great-great-great-great-great-great-great-great-great-grandpa. Thirteen times great!

She, Judy Moody, imagined taking her place on that ruler. She wrote in her name, Judy the Great, right next to Catherine the Great, Isabella of Spain and Nefertiti. Move over, Queen Elizabeth I! Make room for Judy Moody, Y.Q.E. Youngest Queen Ever. Oh, wait. Mary, Queen of Scots, was queen when she was

only six days old. The Famous Women Rulers ruler did not lie.

Mary, Queen of Babies.

But still.

Judy held her head straight. She held her head high. She put on the cardboard crown, sparkling with stick-on gems. She carried her Famous Women Rulers ruler like a royal sceptre. She practiced floating across the room like a queen.

Judy sat on her throne (aka window seat) in the Royal House of Moody. She leaned back, closed her eyes and became a queen.

She, Judy Moody, Queen of Moodovia, lived in a castle with seventy-eight bathrooms that had swan-shaped

baths. It had 7,000 famous paintings, a movie theatre, and her very own personal money machine, not to mention the crown jewels. She swam in the royal pool all day and played with the royal dogs and did cartwheels through the palace gardens with fountains that spouted chocolate.

She was in a royal purple on-top-of-spaghetti-and-the-London-Eye mood!

Judy couldn't wait to tell her teacher, Mr Todd! She was going to have the best family tree in the history of Class 3T. For sure and absolute positive.

Dear Your Majesty

Judy Moody was feeling purpler than a princess. Like a queen! Under her bed, she found the royal purple T-shirt she had gotten all the way from for-real England. It had a crown on it and said KEEP CALM AND CARRY ON. Judy took out her best permanent marker and added LIKE A QUEEN.

Her heart stepped up a beat. Keep

calm and carry on? How could she keep calm when she had just found out she was related to a queen?

Judy could not wait to write to the queen and break the good news. She could not wait to tell her they were almost cousins!

Stink came home from karate. "Why is your hair purple? Is that snail snot? Or were you using my zombie stuff?"

"Stink, guess what. I'm practically a queen! Ask Grandma Lou."

"Grandma Lou had to go home," said Stink.

"Well, she told me our name goes back to old-timey England and I'm related to Queen Elizabeth the First. No lie!"

"Queens got their heads chopped off. No thanks."

"For your information, a queen gets to live in a castle and drink tea and play Monopoly all day and boss people around and own as many dogs as she wants. And she doesn't have to do homework. Ever."

"Well if you're royal, then I am, too."

"Yeah, a royal *pain.*"

"Hardee-har-har," said Stink.

"I wish so bad I had a lucky sixpence for every time you said that, Stinkerbell."

Before Judy could start her letter to the queen, Mum called, "Lunch!" Judy duct-taped a construction-paper tail of peacock feathers to the back of a kitchen chair. "From now on, this will be the royal chair. Like a throne. Only *I* get to sit in it."

She hung a sign on the back of the chair.

QUEEN JUDY'S ROYAL CHAIR

SIT AT YOUR OWN RISK

(THAT MEANS YOU, STINK), OR:

1. Be banished to the Tower of Moody (aka the attic)

2. Polish the royal silver

3. Off with your head

Judy sat upon her throne. "Mum, Dad, we need to talk."

"Uh-oh," said Mum.

"Uh-oh," said Dad. "What did we do now?" he teased.

"Since I'm a royal now, I should have two birthdays. The queen's birthday is in April, like mine, but she has another birthday with a big fat party in the summer."

"I think I see where this is going," said Dad.

"We could celebrate my real birthday in April. Then, in summer, we could have a *second* giant party with a parade and fireworks and pony rides and a bouncy castle. Did I say fireworks? Maybe we could even fire a cannon. What do you say?"

"Then I get two birthdays, too!" said Stink.

"I think one birthday is plenty for an eight-year-old," said Mum.

"Not even if we skip the cannon?" Judy asked.

"Not even," said Dad.

Judy slumped back in her throne. "Can we at least have the Drooping of the Colours?"

"I think it's *Trooping* the Colour," said Mum.

"What's that?" asked Stink.

"You fly a lot of flags," said Judy. She held up a British toothpick flag and waved it half-heartedly.

"If I can't have two birthdays," said Judy, "how about I get a nanny? Someone like Mary Poppins to teach me stuff. She could come live with us and I'd call her 'Miss' and we'd sing all the time and

have tea parties on the
ceiling and fly around on
her umbrella. Her *brolly*, I
mean."

"Who knows," said Mum,
"maybe a magic English nanny
will get blown by the east wind right over
to 117 Croaker Road."

"Okay, okay," said Judy. "But can we
at least have jam pennies? Those teeny-
tiny sandwiches with the crusts cut off?
That's what the Queen eats at teatime."

"What's so great about being related to
a queen anyway?" asked Stink. "I mean,
it's not like we get to live in a castle or
swim in a moat or something."

"Or something," said Judy. "But we

had a royal cousin who was locked up in the Tower of London, Stink. No lie."

Stink bolted up in his seat. "Wait! What?"

Dad explained. "A long time ago, the Moody name was Modig. Somewhere along the way the name got spelled Mudeye. Your grandpa Jack traced him back to the Tower of London. But we don't exactly know why he was there."

"Mudeye Moody!" said Stink. "Hey, that sounds like a pirate name. What if we had a cousin who was a real pirate? I bet a mean queen locked him up in the tower because he wouldn't give up all his loot."

Stink dashed upstairs and came back

wearing his pirate eye patch. "Avast, ye mateys! Hand over your loot." He pretended to steal Judy's candy necklace.

Judy pushed back her royal chair. "I

have a letter to write. I mean – I must catch up on my royal correspondence post-haste."

"Sounds official," said Mum.

"It is! I'm writing to my cousin, the Queen of England, to tell her who I am." Judy searched through the pencil mug on the kitchen counter. "Where's my purple pen? All letters to a queen should be written in purple."

"I don't see why purple is the colour of kings and queens," said Stink. "Don't they know it comes from snail snot?"

"Does not," said Judy.

"I saw it on the Olden Days Channel. The first time they invented the colour purple, it was made from snail slime."

"Sometimes you know the weirdest stuff, Stink."

"Thanks!" said Stink.

❧   ❧   ❧

Upstairs, Judy opened the box with all the stuff from England that Tori had sent.

A teapot. The Shaun the Sheep movie. A London Bridge eraser and Big Ben eraser. A Union Jack flag. The London Underground game. A Where's Wally? colouring book. A Sugar packet collection.

Voilà! Judy would not only write a letter to the Queen. She would send her a sugar packet. A sugar packet for her tea. A sugar packet with a British flag on it.

Judy popped her gum and chewed on this: *What in the world do you say to a queen?* Finally, she ripped a sheet of paper from her notebook. A letter to the Queen had to look *posh*. She decorated it with some glitter glue and a drawing of a queen.

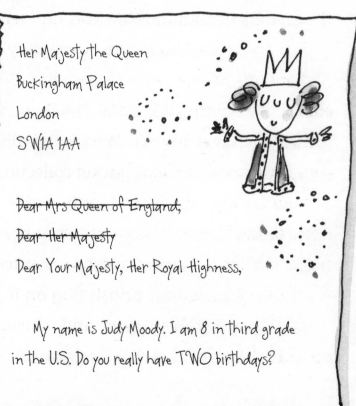

Her Majesty the Queen
Buckingham Palace
London
SW1A 1AA

~~Dear Mrs Queen of England,~~
~~Dear Her Majesty~~
Dear Your Majesty, ~~Her Royal Highness,~~

My name is Judy Moody. I am 8 in third grade in the U.S. Do you really have TWO birthdays?

I only have one and it is April 1. No fooling! My teacher is Mr Todd and we are making family trees. Guess what? I found out we're related! No lie! I thought you'd want to know. (That's a contraction.)

I have a brother named Stink (aka Sir Stinks-A-Lot) and a mum and a dad and a Grandma Lou. She had a ghost in her junk room but it turned out to be a drum set. I like playing drums and reading Nancy Drew and I'm in the Toad Pee Club. Sometimes I get in a bad mood. I have a cat named Mouse and a Venus fly trap named Jaws.

Enough about me! I have some questions 4 U:

1. Are you a good speller? I am N-O-T.

2. True or false: You like to eat eel pie.

3. Can you make someone bring you a snowball in the middle of summer?

4. How many hats do you have?

5. Is your crown heavy?

6. Can you really change a spark plug?

7. I heard you like pigeon races. Say hi to your bird, Sandringham Lightning.

8. How does it feel to be on a sugar packet?

9. Did you ever ride a hinny? (That's a cross between a horse and donkey, not a hiney.) I did.

It's okay if you can't answer all my questions but maybe your Lady-in-Waiting can? (I read that you have 14 of them.) If you can't answer them all please-pretty-please answer #2 and #5. I know you write to people when they turn 100 years old, but I hope you will write to me before I'm 100 because I can't wait 92 whole years!!!!

Signed, Yours in Purple,

Judy Moody

Your Majesty's Humble Non-Pirate Cousin from Across the Pond, Judy Moody

P. S. Sorry if I'm not supposed to say hiney in a letter to the queen.

LONG LIVE the QUEEN

J.M.

A Royal Pain

The next week, Class 3T had a whole hour of library time each day to work on family trees. Judy drew branches on her family tree using her Famous Women Rulers ruler. She cut out sticky notes in the shape of acorns.

"My family tree is going to be lift-the-flap," Judy told Rocky and Frank. "When you lift up each acorn, you find out about the person under it."

"Neat-o!" said Frank. Frank was making a cardboard Christmas tree for his family tree. And Rocky was hanging family photos from a real-live tree branch.

Mr Todd came over to take a peek. "Good work," he said. "Very creative."

"What happens when we're done?" asked Judy.

"You'll each get a chance to tell the class something surprising about your family history," said Mr Todd. "Then we'll display the finished trees in the library."

"Like a family-tree forest," said Judy. "Wicked!"

Jessica Finch came over to Judy's table. "I made a bad goof," she said. "Does anybody have an eraser?"

Judy held out her London Bridge eraser and her Big Ben eraser. "Pick one. But don't use it all up. These are like the crown jewels of my eraser collection."

"I'll take the pink one," said Jessica. *Of course.*

"Don't forget to give it back," said Judy. Sometimes Jessica Finch was an E.E.S. Evil Eraser Stealer.

"Check it out," said Rocky, holding up an old photo. "This is my great-great-grandpa. He searched for gold at the Cripple Creek gold mine."

Judy squinted at the photo. "What's he doing?"

"Um. He's either panning for gold or making soup."

Frank nodded. "I have a great-grandpa from the Middle Ages who sold either pears or pearls."

"So your name could have been Frank *Pear* instead of Frank Pearl?"

"I know, right?" Frank cracked up. "And I have another great-grandpa who was in a famous shipwreck on the *Lusitania*."

"Same-same!" said Judy. "I have some-body that went down on the *Titanic*!"

"Mine escaped in a lifeboat," said Frank.

"That's brill," Judy said.

"Huh?" said Rocky and Frank at the same time.

"She means brilliant," said Jessica, butting in again. "It's like wicked. It's how you say excellent or awesome in England."

"Don't get your knickers in a twist," said Judy. "See, my family tree is from England. I learned funny British words from Tori, my pen pal. She lives in London."

"I see London. I see France..." said Frank.

"You do?" Judy flushed red. She checked to see if her underwear was showing.

"Made you look!" said Frank.

"Good one," said Judy.

"You better go to the loo and check," said Jessica. "Just in case."

"The loo?" asked Rocky.

"The who?" asked Frank.

"The bathroom," Judy whispered.

Judy looked in the mirror, front and back. *Phew!* No sign of undies. She brushed eraser crumbs off of her KEEP CALM AND CARRY ON T-shirt. *Wait just a Big Ben minute. How did Jessica A. Finch know so much British stuff?*

Judy plopped back down at their table. She made sure Jessica could hear.

"My great-great-great-great-great-great-great-great-great-great-great-great-great-grandpa was related to a queen. Queen Elizabeth the First of England. Just think – maybe he was the queen's royal brother or something. She probably put him in charge of the crown jewels at the Tower of London. So you are looking at a queen!"

Rocky hung another photo from a branch. Frank peeled dried glue from his hand. "Hey, look, I'm shedding."

"Hel–lo! Don't you get it? I have royal blood. I'm related to the Queen of England. I could, like, be invited to a sleepover at the palace or something."

"Cool," said Rocky.

"Cool," said Frank.

"You mean *wicked,*" said Jessica, turning around. Nosy Parker. Snoopy McSnoop.

"Guys," said Judy. "We're talking castles, moats, Big Ben, Buckingham Palace, the Tower of London!" Frank's eyes bugged out.

"You mean where all those people—" Rocky drew an imaginary line across his neck—"got their heads chopped off?"

"Yah-huh. It holds the crown jewels – some of the biggest diamonds in the world. And it used to have a zoo with lions and tigers and a polar bear and alligators and about a hundred rattlesnakes. Six ravens still guard the tower at all times."

"And they had a lioness named Elizabeth," said Jessica.

Judy gaped at Jessica. How did Jessica Know-It-All Finch know this?

"What?" said Jessica. "I overheard you talking about the Tower of London. So, when the lioness died, everybody thought Queen Elizabeth was going to die, too. But you probably knew that."

Jessica Queen Bee Finch knew about queens, too?

Judy held out her hand. "Eraser. Can I have it back, please?"

"You mean *rubber*?" Jessica handed it back. Two of the bridge towers were worn to nubs. Sometimes Jessica A. Finch was *beastly*.

"London Bridge is falling down," said Rocky.

The Mood Sapphire

On Saturday, Judy taped a British flag on her door. "The queen flies a flag when she's in the palace. So if you see this flag, Stink, it means I'm in my room."

The doorbell rang. "Judy!" Mum called up the stairs. "Grandma Lou's here."

Judy took down the flag and ran downstairs.

"Grandma Lou," said Judy. "What are you doing here?" She gave her grandma a great big fat hug. "Ouch!" Judy cried, pulling away to see what felt scratchy.

Judy could not believe her royal green eyes. Her royal mouth fell open.

Grandma Lou was wearing a long fuzzy sweater. On the front of her royal purple sweater was a peacock. Not just any old peacock. A peacock with all the colours of the ocean and a tail made of jewels. And there, right in the centre of the peacock's tail, was the brightest, shiningest, sparklingest jewel Judy had ever seen.

It was as blue as the Star of India. It was as green as the Patricia Emerald. It was as sparkly as the Hope Diamond. The crown jewel of the Royal House of Moody, right here in her very own living room.

Un-believe-a-bling!

"What is it, Jelly Bean?" asked Grandma Lou.

"Your peacock pin," said Judy. "It's like those fancy jewels in the queen's crown. Shouldn't it be in a museum or something?"

Grandma Lou laughed. "This old thing? I came across it when I was looking for the Moody crest to help you with your family tree project." She took it off and held it out for Judy to see. "It's just junk jewellery. I think I got it at a bazaar when I was in the Peace Corps in India."

"It's like those world-famous jewels Stink and I saw in that hall of rocks. At the Museum of Natural History."

Stink bounced down the stairs. "Let me see!" He wormed his way past Judy. "Whoa," he said in a hush.

"It looks like a star that fell right out of the sky," said Judy.

"Did you know the Star of India is the world's largest star sapphire?" said Stink. "It's like two billion years old. No lie."

"Interesting," said Grandma Lou.

"And the Patricia Emerald is this big green stone and it has twelve sides and it was named after a girl."

"I'd sure like to see that someday," said Grandma Lou. She handed Judy a folder. "I just stopped by to drop off these pictures of the Moody family crest. It might give you some ideas."

"Aren't you going to stay?" asked Judy.

"Not today, Jelly Bean. I'm taking Pugsy to a playdate at the park."

Grandma Lou pinned the peacock on Judy's hoodie. "I hereby bequeath this gem upon you, Your Royal Highness, Judy the Great."

"For real? Wait till Tori hears about this!"

❧　❧　❧

Judy and Stink studied the peacock pin up close. "Sapphires, emeralds, and a diamond for the peacock's eye. It must be a billion years old," said Stink.

Judy shined a torch on the largest stone. "Look at the way it changes colour in the light. Like my mood ring!"

"It's a mood sapphire," said Stink.

"The Royal Moody Sapphire! It's gem-brilliant! Queens are way into peacocks, you know. Peacocks are a symbol of royalty, Stink. Maybe it belonged to a queen."

Stink's eyes sparkled like gemstones. "What if this was from Mudeye Moody's secret stash of pirate booty? Maybe he hid it on a desert island. Then when he escaped, he dug it up."

"Yeah! Then he sailed around the world on the seven oceans and a pirate's monkey stole it and carried it off. But the monkey dropped it in the ocean and a fish swallowed it."

"Then they found it inside the fish!" said Stink, clapping his hands.

"So maybe *that's* how it made its way to a street fair in India, where Grandma Lou found it again after hundreds of years," Judy said. "Who knew when I started a family tree that we'd find the Moody crown jewels?"

The room got quiet. Gobsmacked quiet. "You know what this needs, Stink? A place of honour. A special safe place where we can admire it any time we want."

"Like a Moody museum?"

"Exactly," said Judy. "Follow me, Stinker. I have a right-royal-rare idea."

Judy led the way to the Toad Pee tent in the backyard. She pinned the crown jewel of the Royal House of Moody to a fancy pillow. She placed the pillow of honour in the centre of the Toad Pee tent. "Behold the Royal Moody Sapphire."

Judy and Stink stood in awe. They were starstruck, Star-of-India-struck, just gazing at the crown jewel of the Royal House of Moody.

After they gazed at the bedazzling jewel for one whole minute – which felt like a fortnight – Judy broke the spell by tugging at Stink's arm.

She pulled him outside the tent. "Stand there, Stinkerbell. You are officially an official member of the official queen's guard."

"I am?"

"It's official," said Judy.

Stink started to slump. He scratched his head. He dug his toe in the dirt.

"Stand up straight, Stink. Stop fidgeting." Judy put a black top hat on Stink's head. "This will be your uniform, like the guards at the Tower of London wear."

The hat came down over Stink's eyes. He laughed. "I can't see!"

"Stand still. The queen's guards do not wriggle. They barely even blink. And they definitely do not giggle."

"No wriggling. No giggling. Got it." Stink giggled.

"You're giggling right now, Stinker. This is a very important job. You hold the keys and protect the priceless jewels."

Judy told Stink about the way-official Ceremony of the Keys and what to say.

"Halt! Who goes there?" said Stink.

"The keys!" said Judy.

"Whose keys?"

"The queen's keys."

"Pass the queen's keys," said Stink. "All is well."

"Rare!" said Judy. "Now remember,

Stinkerbell, no matter what happens, you stand there and guard, okay?"

Stink nodded.

"No nodding!" said Judy. Stink held his head statue-still. He tried not to blink.

"Cheerio!" Judy waved as she went back into the house. She munched on a banana. She read *The Trumpet of the Swan*. She played hide-and-seek with Mouse. She drew a knight's head at the top of the Moody crest. She drew peacock feathers around a shield. She drew a pirate, a crown, a ship, and a lioness inside the shield.

Seconds went by. Minutes. An hour. Judy wrote a snail-mail letter to Tori. She watched some telly and played tic-tac-toe with Mouse and put on her pj's and got ready for *Bed*fordshire. She zonked out in no time.

"Hey, anybody?" called Stink without moving his head. "How long do I have to stand out here, anyway?"

Fish Farts and Swan Songs

The next morning, Judy was dig-dig-digging in the dirt around the Toad Pee tent.

"What are you doing?"

"Digging." *Puff, puff, puff.*

"Digging what?"

"I'm making a moat around the Toad Pee tent, Stink." *Puff, puff.*

"Why?"

"To protect the Moody crown jewels. *Somebody* was supposed to stand guard

outside the T. P. tent. *Somebody* was supposed to guard the Royal Moody Sapphire. But *somebody* left his post."

"Somebody got hungry," said Stink. "And tired."

"Royal guards do not sleep, Stink. Or eat." She handed Stink a shovel. Stink started digging. *Puff, puff.*

"The moat is going to hold all the fishes royal, too."

"Fishes royal?"

"The Queen of England loves animals. She's had more than thirty palace dogs in her lifetime. And she owns *all* the fish in the water around England."

"For real?" Stink dug some more. *Puff, puff, puff.*

"For real. She even owns all the swans in the River Thames."

"What about whales?"

"Yep. Them too. And porpoises and dolphins and—"

"What about tuna fish?"

"*All* the fish, Stink."

"Even stinky sushi?" asked Stink.

"Even stinky sushi."

Stink stopped digging. He tossed down his shovel. "I'm tired of digging."

"But you hardly—"

"I'm going over to Webster's for a thumb-wrestling match."

"Fine," said Judy. "But don't think when you come home all sweaty you're going to swim in my moat!"

꩜   ꩜   ꩜

When Stink came home from Webster's house, he ran outside to see the moat. Judy lay on her tummy, staring into a puddle.

Something was floating in the puddle! Something shiny. Something red and purple. Something with fan-like fins and a floaty tail. Something that looked an awful-lot-exactly like Stink's Siamese fighting fish!

"Is that...?" asked Stink, leaning over to peer into the puddle.

"That's my royal fish," said Judy.

"That's *my* royal fish!" cried Stink.

"His name is Prince Redmond the First," said Judy.

"His name is Spike," said Stink. "He's *my* Siamese fighting fish that I got at Fur & Fangs with *my* leftover Tooth Fairy money! You stole him."

"I didn't nick him, Stink," said Judy. "I took him by royal decree!" She swept her arm through the air. "I own all the fishes in the kingdom."

"I want my fish back."

"It's for the greater good, Stink. So the whole queendom can enjoy him." Judy pointed to spit bubbles on the water. "Look, Prince Redmond the First already made a bubble nest."

"Guess what," said Stink. "Did you know fish communicate by farting?"

"No way," said Judy.

"It's true," said Stink. "Spike is probably breaking wind right now."

"Royal fish don't fart, Stink."

Judy watched more bubbles rise to the surface. Stink leaned over to listen. "Spike is saying, 'Give me back to Stink!'"

"Fine." Judy scooped Prince Redmond the Farter into a yogurt container and handed him back to Stink. "A farting fish is not fit for a queen anyway."

"Hello, Spiky-Spike-Spike," Stink cooed.

Where-oh-where could she get a royal fish?

Judy went down to the creek to look. She knew all about critters in creeks from her after-school Creek Freaks Club. She saw minnows. She saw water striders. She saw common netspinner caddis flies. She spotted dragonfly larva. She spotted beetle larva. She even scooped up a water-penny beetle.

She tried to catch a minnow, but it slipped away too fast.

If only she had a royal swan!

She, Judy Moody, was the queen of no one. The boss of nothing. Not even a farting fish. Not even a minnow.

Just then, she, Judy Moody, got a gob-smacking-great idea.

Maybe, just maybe, she could get a swan to come to her! A trumpeter swan, just like Louis in *The Trumpet of the Swan.*

Judy dug out her *Backyard Becky* magazines. *Backyard Becky* said swans ate birdseed. Judy dumped a bag of birdseed all around her moat. *Backyard Becky* said swans liked the colour red. Judy put out a pile of red things – a red bucket, a red boot, a red ball. *Backyard Becky* said swans called to each other.

"*Hoo! Hoo! Ko-HOH! Hoo!*" Judy sang a swan song. But no swan came.

Backyard Becky even told how to weave a nest for a swan. *Start with a Hula-Hoop. Using wool, weave back and forth in a simple monkey chain knot.* Judy ran to get her Hula-Hoop. She wove her finger-knitting chain back and forth to make a nest.

From inside the house, she waited, watching the backyard.

"A watched pot never boils," said Mum.

"It's going to take time for a swan to find your nest," said Dad.

Judy gave it time. She gave it more time. She gave it time until it was time for *Bed*fordshire. She gave it time all the way until the next morning. As soon as she woke up, she ran to her window seat and peered into the backyard.

Something was floating on her moat! Most excellent!

Was it a swan? A trumpeter swan? Maybe it was a whooper swan, like in her *Backyard Becky* magazine. Or a whistling swan. Or a black-necked swan.

She peered through her periscope. It had a short neck. It most definitely was *not* a swan.

Was it an … ugly duckling? Judy hurried outside. She tiptoed across the back deck. She crawled across the grass until she got close enough to see.

It was not a swan. It was not a bird. It was a duck.

A rubber duck!

And the rubber ducky was wearing a crown.

Stink crawled out of the Toad Pee tent. "Stink! Check it out!" said Judy. "A royal rubber ducky!"

"How did *that* get there?" asked Stink, wide-eyed.

"No clue," said Judy. "But it's mine. Look, it even has a crown. Just like the queen's rubber ducky."

"What do you mean?" Stink asked.

"The Queen of England has a rubber ducky in the royal bathroom. No lie. And her rubber ducky has a crown, too."

Stink could not believe his ears. "No way!"

"Way!" said Judy. "Jessica told me. A painter was painting the royal bathroom when he spotted it. He told all the news-papers in England. That's called a leak, Stink."

"The royal bathroom sprang a leak!" said Stink. They cracked up.

"By order of the British Empire, I

hereby decree that I, Queen Judy, have dominion over *all* bath toys in the state of Virginia! Not just rubber ducks."

"Not all," said Stink. "Some are mine."

"But you don't play with bath toys anymore, right?" Judy asked. "Too babyish."

"R–right."

Judy held out her hand. "Then hand over your squirting submarine, Stink."

"Tubmarine? Never!"

H.M.R.R.S.
Her Majesty's Right Royal Spies

Now that Judy was a royal, she was dying to see a castle. There were nine castles in Virginia, but only one looked anything like Buckingham Palace – the queen's house in England (where Judy *should* be living).

Family field trip time!

She, Judy Moody, was on her way to a castle. Not a sand castle. Not a bouncy castle. A castle-castle! For real and absolute positive.

"This is it," said Dad. "Wolff Castle." Everybody piled out of the car. A high fence was built around the big mansion with a gate and a tower at each corner.

"Does it have a dungeon?" Stink asked.

"That's *your* bedroom, Stink," said Judy, cracking herself up.

"It's kind of small for a castle," said Stink.

"I'd like to live in a house this small," Mum teased.

"Do you think it's for sale? Maybe we could live here," said Judy.

"In your dreams," said Dad, laughing.

"Where's the moat?" asked Stink. "What about a drawbridge? Where's the place where they chop off people's heads?"

The Moodys walked through rose gardens and up red-carpeted stairs. They entered a long hallway lined with marble statues and shining suits of armour. A grand staircase rose in the centre. Crystal chandeliers sparkled so brightly that Cinderella's stepsisters would have gasped in wonder.

Judy spun around in awe. "Wow, I've never seen so much shiny stuff."

"Even the lights are made of diamonds," said Stink.

The castle had a secret staircase and

a hidden tunnel. They toured room after room after room full of giant mirrors and stained-glass windows, claw-footed furniture and gold-painted ceilings. Even the doorknobs were fancy.

"Who lived here?" asked Stink.

"Some guy from England," said Judy. "He built it for all his books and his art." She leaned across a rope to peer into a bedroom with purple velvet drapes. The bed had twenty-some purple pillows. "This could be my room," she told Stink.

In every room, Stink asked, "Is this where they chopped off heads?"

"Stink," said Judy, "stop saying that or they'll send *you* to the tower."

"What should we do first?" Judy asked. "There's a falcon show, rowboats on the lake, and a royal tea party. I call tea party."

"Falcons!" said Stink.

"Rowboats," said Dad.

Mum was frowning. "I'm afraid we didn't get tickets ahead of time. The events are all sold out."

"There's some sort of maze to find a corgi," said Dad. But the maze turned out to be a boring-old worksheet. And the corgi was just a drawing. Lame–o!

"We still haven't seen the throne room," said Mum.

"Or the hall of kings and queens," said Dad.

Judy and Stink stepped into a long hall lined with paintings of kings and queens. Each one had a story.

"King Henry the Second liked to read before he went to bed. Just like me!" said Stink. "And this guy, King Edward the First, had long legs, so they called him Long Shanks."

"The queen dubs 3,500 people a year to be knights. I hereby dub you Short Shanks," said Judy.

"*Sir* Short Shanks." Stink read the tag next to the painting of a guy in a red robe and pointy slippers. "Says here Richard the Second owned the first hankie. What's a hankie?"

"It's a cloth you use to blow your nose. Like fancy toilet paper. Right, Mum?"

Mum laughed. "I guess you could say that."

"Where's Richard the Turd?" asked Stink.

Judy cracked up. "You said *turd*."

"*Third*. I said *Third*."

"Here's Henry the Eighth," said Dad. "He had six different wives."

"Two of them got their heads chopped off," said Stink.

"Here's poor Lady Jane Grey," said Judy. "She only got to be queen for nine days."

"Did they chop off her head?" Stink asked.

"No, Stink. Some queens got to keep their heads."

"Here's Queen Elizabeth the First," said Mum. "That's who Virginia is named for."

"Why are her teeth black?" Judy asked.

"They rotted from too many sweets," said Mum.

"Ew," said Judy.

"Queen Victoria always wore black," said Mum. "It says she had a royal chauffeur, a royal rat catcher, and a royal bug destroyer." *Zap! Zap!* Stink leaped through the hall, pretending to catch bugs.

In the throne room, Stink tried out two different thrones.

"Hey, Short Shanks, over here." Judy pointed to the crest on one of the thrones. It had a shield in the middle with a knight's head and feathers around it. In the centre were two arms holding a rose and a big letter *M* at the bottom.

"It looks just like our family crest," said Judy.

"The *M* is for *Moody*!" said Stink.

"Or *Mudeye*," said Judy.

"Yeah. That old name for Moody."

"Stink, pretend I'm the queen, and you be the Royal Poet."

"Why can't I be queen?" asked Stink.

"Fine," said Judy. "You be queen. I'll be the Royal Poet." She took a bow. "Your Majesty. I brought you a spot of tea. Oh fiddle-dee-dee. I spilled it on your knee. How terribly klutzy of me."

"Hey, you rhyme."

"Of course, silly horse. The Royal Poet speaks in rhyme. All the time."

"I want to be Royal Poet! I just didn't know it." Stink and Judy cracked up.

At the end of the hall was a secret room. In the secret room was a painting. "Look," said Judy. "You can peek through the eyes of the painting!"

Stink stood on tiptoe. He put his eyes up to the holes in the painting. He could see through to the next room.

"We're royal spies!" said Judy. "What's it like in there?"

"It's flowerful. Looks like a bunch of

kids at some kind of tea party thing. Wait a second. Isn't that … I think I see…"

"No fair, Short Shanks. Quit hogging. My turn." Judy peeked through the painting. She could not believe her royal spying eyes.

Judy was peering into a flower-covered room with a long table, a froufrou table-cloth, and fancy teacups. High tea! And seated at the table, wearing a puffy pink dress, long white gloves, and a tiara was none other than…

Jessica Fink Finch!

Blimey! It was *her* all right. Judy would know that tiara-wearing Queen Bee of Spelling anywhere.

"What's *she* doing here?" asked Stink.

"Drinking tea." Royal tea. High tea. Tea probably made of royal rose petals. Tea that she, Judy Moody, was not drinking.

Jessica Finch got to drink tea in a for-real castle! Jessica Finch got to eat coronation chicken and crown-shaped cookies. Jessica Finch got to play a royal game of charades.

It was *so* not fair. Judy was the one related to a queen, not Jessica.

Suddenly, she, Judy Moody, had an idea. A smashing idea! She would throw a right royal tea party of her own, and invite her friends. The invitations would be written in super-secret spy code, so Jessica A. Finch would never know.

Maybe Dad would let her get a bouncy castle. Maybe Mum would let her use dishes, the kind that can break for real. Not paper plates and cups.

It was going to be a big-deal do. A tea party fit for a queen. And the crowning Mument would be when she, Judy Mud-eye Moody, was crowned queen, with all her loyal friends around her. She could see it now…

Sir Short Shanks stood on tiptoe. "What are they saying?"

"Shh. I'm trying to hear," Judy spy-whispered.

Jessica curtsied. "My favourite part of the castle was the chair in the throne room," she told the kids at the table.

"The one with the knight's head and the letter *M*."

The royal Moody chair!

Judy almost choked. "HEY! That's *our* chair. The one with the *M*-for-*Moody* crest. Not *F*-for-*Finch*."

Something was not right. Something was hinky. Something was wonky. Jessica Finch sure was annoying. Now she knew how the queen felt when somebody forgot to curtsy. B-u-g-g-e-d!

"Time to go," Mum and Dad called. Last stop: gift shop. Judy got her very own hankie. Stink got a deck of cards with facts about doomed kings and queens.

Short Shanks spouted fun facts all the way home. "Did you know George the First died of eating too many strawberries? Anne Boleyn had an extra finger! Henry the Eighth played tennis while his wife's head was getting chopped off."

All Judy could think about was Jessica Finch and the royal Moody chair. *Roar!* She felt like a queen all right – a scream queen. If Jessica had copied her family tree, heads were going to roll.

Stugly Upsisters

Friday was going to be the best school day ever. It was the day that Class 3T would be sharing their family trees. By the end of today, the whole school and the whole entire world would find out that she, Judy Moody, was related to a queen.

Before school started, Judy passed out invitations to her tea party. They were written in secret code. Code that only Mary, Queen of Scots, could crack.

But that didn't stop Jessica Fink Finch.

Before Judy could tell her friends where the answer key was hidden, Jessica Finch pulled out a Wolff Castle gift-shop pocket code-cracker. She cracked the royal code. So much for top-secret.

"A party!" said Frank.

"*Tea* party," said Judy.

"Do we get to throw tea in your bath, like we did at the Boston Tub Party?"

"I'll do magic tricks," said Rocky.

"Let's have a race," said Amy Namey. "I can announce the winner in my newspaper."

"No, no, and no," said Judy. Sometimes her friends were such plebes. "You guys don't get it, because you are not related to a queen, like I am. This is a right royal tea party."

"So what *do* we get to do?" asked Frank.

"Sip tea and practice manners and learn to curtsy," said Jessica.

"You get to eat stuff like crumb cakes," said Judy.

"You mean crumpets," said Jessica.

"All that matters is there will be a coronation, and I will be crowned Queen."

Her friends looked at her like she was starkers. As in cuckoo-crazy!

"How come *you* get to be Queen?" asked Frank.

"I'm the only one with royal blood. Duh."

Just then, the bell rang. Judy's friends rushed to class. "Hey, wait up!"

But nobody waited up.

Judy hurried after them. "There will be a bouncy castle!" It wasn't true. It was a big fat lie. But she had to make a tea party sound exciting somehow.

So far, so bad. The best school day

ever was a royal flop. But pretty soon the world would find out that Judy Moody was related to a hero, and maybe a pirate, and almost-for-sure a queen.

Family tree time! Judy raised her hand to go first. Mr Todd called on Madison and Addison. He called on Manuel and Isabel. He called on Rocky. He called on Frank Pear/Pearl.

Judy was at sixes and sevens. Eights and nines, too. Then it happened. Her teacher called on none other than Jessica Fink Finch.

Jessica Finch stood in front of the class. Jessica Finch wore her posh tea party dress. Jessica Finch pulled on long white gloves. She put on pearls that were not

a candy necklace and placed her Queen Bee tiara on her head.

Jessica Finch did not look like a fink. She looked like a princess. She looked like Cinderella herself. Judy pulled her candy necklace out from under her shirt. She snuck a secret bite. *Chomp.* At least Jessica Finch did not have a crown-jewel mood-changing peacock pin.

Jessica traced her Finch family tree back to merry olde England. Hey! Judy Moody's family tree went back to merry olde England, too. Same-same!

Jessica Finch told the class that way back in time the name Finch used to be Fink. Ha! So Jessica Finch actually *was* a fink. For real and absolute positive! *Well, I'll be gobsmacked!*

Then Jessica Finch held up her family crest. It had a giant *M* on it. Judy's family crest had a giant *M* on it, too. *M* was for *Moody.*

Judy's hand shot up. "Um, excuse me. But why does your family crest say *M*? It should say *F* for *Fink.* I mean *Finch.*"

"Hold your crumpets," said Jessica. "I'm getting to that part."

Chomp. Chomp-chomp. Judy was only half listening. Jessica Finch was related to a judge. Bor–ing. Jessica Finch was related to a baron. Snooze. Jessica Finch was related to the third Earl of Blah-Blah. *Zzzzzz.*

Judy bet that Jessica Finch did not have a great-great-uncle on the *Titanic*. Jessica Finch did not have a cousin with a pirate name like Mudeye Moody. Jessica Finch did not have an ancestor who maybe guarded the crown jewels in the for-real Tower of London.

Wait. What? *Titanic*? Suddenly, Judy could not believe her not-listening ears. Did Jessica just say that *she* was related to someone who was on the *Titanic*?

Judy sucked in a breath. No way, no how. Impossible. There was only one explanation. Jessica Finch was a big fat family-tree stealer!

Wait till Judy told Mr Todd. *F*-was-for-*Flunk*. Judy raised her hand Mr Todd asked her to hold her question till the end.

Queens did not wait their turns. Queens did not bite their tongues when family-tree-stealing rat finks told royal lies. Queens threw people like that in the tower.

Now Jessica was telling a story about her ancestors in the olden days of kings and queens. Same-same *again.* Copycat. Copy-kitten. Copy-lioness!

Chomp-chomp-chomp. Three more bites of candy necklace down the hatch.

Judy raised her hand again. Mr Todd frowned.

"Once upon a time," Jessica was saying, "back in ye olde England, the Finch family had a longer name. They were the Mudeye-Finches. That's why my

family crest has an *M*-for-*Mudeye*, not an
F-for-*Finch*."

Mudeye! Did she say Mudeye? Mudeye
was an old-timey name for Moody.

Judy knew her family tree by heart.
Her family name was once spelled Modig,
then Mudeye, then Moody. How could
Jessica Finch have the name Mudeye,
too?

"Mr Todd!" Judy jumped up out of her
seat.

"Judy, please keep your seat," said Mr
Todd. "I don't want to tell you again."

To make matters worse, Jessica was
telling a story about the Tower of London.
Now Mr Todd would think *she* was the
copycat!

"My ancestor was Lady Philberta Finch," said Jessica. "She raised songbirds for Queen Victoria. Then one day, one of the royal finches pooped ... right on the queen's head!" Class 3T laughed like crazy.

"Poor Philberta got locked up in the Tower of London."

Judy wanted this to be over. "The end!" Judy shouted.

"Judy," said Mr Todd. "I'm going to have to ask you to move to Antarctica."

"But...!" Her teapot was about to boil. *Keep calm and carry on ... to Antarctica.*

Judy slunk to the desk in the back of the room with a map of Antarctica. She glared at the cardboard penguin holding the CHILL OUT sign.

The rest of Class 3T was on the edge of their seats. "What happened to the lady who got locked in the tower?" asked Frank.

"Did they chop off her head?" asked Rocky.

"Nope. She got rescued by a brave lad who went by the name of Mudeye."

GULP!

"Was he a prince?" asked Addison and Madison at the same time.

"Yes!" said Judy before she knew what she was saying.

"No," said Jessica. "Mudeye wasn't a prince at all. He wasn't even royal. He was the royal *rat catcher* – the guy who caught the rats in the Tower of London."

Rat fink! Jessica had to be talking rubbish. Telling tall tales! Jessica should be sent to Antarctica for lying like a rug. Jessica should be banished to the Tower. The Tower of No Talking. The Tower of No Tea Parties.

"Then what happened?" Class 3T asked.

"This Mudeye guy helped her escape from the Tower and they fell in love and ran away together and that's how they became the Mudeye-Finches."

Class 3T started clapping.

"Decades later their kids and kids' kids sailed for America. That's how my family first came to this country. But it was too hard to say Mudeye-Finch all the time, so Mudeye got dropped and our name was just Finch. The end."

The end of Judy and the Royal House of Moody.

Pinkie Swear

Class 3T went wild, standing and clapping even more. Jessica Finch curtsied.

Judy Moody did not stand up. Judy Moody did not clap. Judy Moody put her head down on the South Pole. She wanted to cry into her not-royal hankie.

Jessica Finch always did her homework. Jessica Finch always got big fat A's, except for when they were A-pluses. Her family tree did not lie.

If Jessica Finch was telling the truth, then her great-grandpa-times-thirteen was NOT related to a queen after all.

She, Judy Moody, was more rat than royal.

She was not from a long line of blue bloods. She was not from a long line of queens. She was not even a teeny tiny bit like Cinderella. She was from a long line of rat catchers. The lowliest of the low. Royal rat catchers were worse than royal bug squishers.

Then it hit her like a ship crashing into an iceberg. This was titanic!

If Jessica's story was true, then she, Judy Mudeye Moody, was related to... Jessica Fink Finch!

If you went way, way, way, way, way back in the family tree, Jessica Finch was Judy Moody's long lost ... *stepsister*?

Blimey! Judy's knickers were in a right Piccadilly of a twist.

Forget Cinderella. She and Jessica were the stugly upsisters. Ugly stepsisters!

Judy wanted to float away on an Antarctic iceberg to a land Far Far Away.

She looked down at her KEEP CALM

T-shirt. It should say KEEP CALM AND CARRY ON LIKE A ROYAL RAT CATCHER.

"Earth to Judy," said Mr Todd.

It was *finally* her turn, but she didn't care. She couldn't stand in front of her friends and her whole class and tell them that she was not related to a queen. She was descended from a not-royal, good-for-nothing rat catcher.

"You can return to your seat, Judy. We're out of time for today. We'll pick up with your family tree on Monday."

Phew! Nobody knew her big fat secret yet. Nobody knew that she was an un-queen. And nobody-but-nobody knew that she was secret sort-of-sisters with Jessica Finch. Nobody could ever know.

Judy picked up her Famous Women Rulers ruler. She could no longer read her name there, it was so smudged. She snuck a bite of candy necklace. They were no longer pearls.

All of a sudden, a note folded like a crown landed on her Social Studies Student Edition Grade Three book.

She looked around. She unfolded the note. *Hi, Sis!!*

Hi, Sis!! Two short words of perfect penmanship. The swirly capital *S*. The smiley-face *i*. The slanty double exclamation points. These were the marks of the Princess of Penmanship. The Queen of Cursive. The Her-Majesty of Handwriting.

Jessica A-Plus Finch.

She knew!

The secret was out. Soon it would be all over Class 3T that Judy Moody was not – I repeat not – related to a queen. It would be all over the whole school that Judy *was* related to Jessica Fink Finch.

Arch-frenemy Jessica Finch had ruined everything. How could Judy have a right royal tea party and be crowned queen if she was not even royal?

Judy glared at the ponytail in front of her. The same ponytail she stared at every day. But today it did not belong to her know-it-all rival. It did not belong to the show-off Queen Bee of Spelling. Today it belonged to her long lost … stepsister!

Stugly upsister, Judy told herself. She

tweaked that ponytail. Once, twice. Jessica turned around. She wasn't even annoyed. She was smiling. Her eyes sparkled like crown jewels.

"Meet me by the lockers," Judy whispered. She headed for the back of the room. Jessica followed.

"You can't tell anybody—" Judy started.

"We're secret stepsisters," said Jessica, jumping up and down.

"Shh!" said Judy.

"But I always wanted a sister," said Jessica.

"Stop saying sister!" said Judy. "You especially can't tell Rocky or Frank or Amy. They'll never come to my party and

crown me queen if they find out I'm not even royal. I'm related to a rat catcher."

"A very *brave* rat catcher!" said Jessica.

"Mudeye *does* mean brave. But even a brave rat catcher is no queen," said Judy. She reached into her pocket. "If you keep this secret, I'll give you my hankie."

"Ew! No thanks," said Jessica.

"My candy necklace?" Judy stretched it out for Jessica to see.

"It's all slobbery. And half-eaten!" said Jessica.

Judy held a pinkie in the air. Not a tea-drinking pinkie. A long-lost-stepsister, swear-on-a-secret pinkie. "Pinkie swear!"

Judy and Jessica locked pinkies. "Lips lock, never talk," they chanted.

"You pinkie swore," said Judy. "You can't tell anyone."

"I'll keep your secret," said Jessica. "On *one* condition."

"Name it," said Judy.

"You have to invite me to your royal tea party. After all, I'm the one with the royal name here."

GULP!

Dayus Horribilus

Judy hopped off the bus and waved good-bye to Rocky and Frank. "Don't forget my party tomorrow. Saturday. T. P. tent. Four o'clock sharp. Look for the bouncy castle!"

Jessica Finch walked home with Judy. She had taken over as Judy's party planner. After all, Jessica had been to a real high tea at an actual castle. Judy had only spied on one.

"So here's the thing," said Judy. "I

promised my friends a bouncy castle. But Mum and Dad won't let me."

"Queens don't bounce anyway," Jessica pointed out. "They don't even break a sweat. Especially not at a tea party."

"What do they do?" asked Judy.

"Drink tea and eat finger sandwiches and pink foods like salmon mousse."

"Moose? Where am I going to get a moose? I can't even get a bouncy castle."

"Mousse is a food. Like pudding. Only it's made of fish."

Fish pudding! That sounded awfully fishy to Judy.

"I think my friends would rather jump in a castle than eat a moose."

"I have an idea," said Jessica. "Leave it to me."

"This is it!" said Judy when they got to the Toad Pee tent out back. "Party Central."

Jessica looked around, thinking. "Make a list." Judy picked up her Grouchy pencil. "We need a table for the tea. Teapot. Tablecloth. Doilies. Napkins."

"Nappies, check," said Judy.

"Not nappies!" said Jessica. "Nap*kins*. Nappies are diapers!"

Judy crossed nappies off the list. She added real dishes.

Jessica was waffling on. "We'll make name cards so everybody knows where to sit. And we'll have three different kinds of tea. Peppermint, Earl Grey…"

"Earl who?"

"Are you writing this down?" asked Jessica. Jessica Finch sure was bossy when it came to tea parties. "We'll have tea first, then the crowning."

"How about party favours?" Judy asked.

"Everyone will get a tea bag and an egg cup to take home."

Tea bags? Egg cups? Judy wasn't so sure her friends were going to like this. But then she pictured herself on a velvet pillow sipping high tea and wearing the Royal Moody Sapphire and getting crowned Queen of Queens.

At last it was Saturday, the day of the right royal tea party. The T. P. tent was hung with twinkly lights and pink bunting (aka paper streamers). The table was set. The place cards were placed. The napkins were folded into swans. The tea was ready to be poured. The Toad Pee tent looked more like the *Total Princess* tent. Even the sugar cubes were pink. Judy sure hoped her friends liked it.

All there was to do now was wait. Wait for four o'clock. Judy chewed her Grouchy pencil. She chewed her fingernail. She chewed the end of her once-purple hair hunk.

Four o'clock came. And went. Nobody was on time.

4:03: Judy checked her watch.

4:05: Judy checked her watch again.

4:07: Judy twisted her swan napkin into a tornado.

"Maybe they got the time wrong," said Judy.

"The invitation said four o'clock sharp," said Jessica.

"But it was in secret code," said Judy.

4:11: Judy folded an origami peacock with her doily.

"It's bad manners to be late," said Jessica. "So rude." She checked and double-checked the sugar bowl.

4:15: Judy folded an origami polar bear with Rocky's doily.

"It's bad manners to keep a queen waiting," said Jessica. She smoothed the tablecloth. She fluffed the napkins. She whipped the P.U. fish pudding.

4:19: Judy folded a camel, a lion and an elephant out of extra doilies. She made a whole royal zoo out of origami.

4:25: *Where is everyone?*

4:37: *Nobody's coming!*

Jessica stopped neatening napkins and fixing forks. Even Jessica Fussy Finch knew it was no use.

"My friends aren't coming," said Judy. *If only Tori did not live all the way across the pond in London.*

She held a right royal tea party and nobody came. Not even Stink! Judy felt like a rat. A lowly rat catcher's daughter times thirteen. How many times had Judy thought of Jessica Finch as a rat fink? But she, Judy Moody, was the real rat. And her friends had finked out on her. Finky-Finkersons!

The finger sandwiches wilted. The

mousse smelled worse than a moose. And the royal tea went cold.

"This is like the Queen's *annus horribilus*!" said Judy. "The terrible year back in 1992 when bad stuff happened – one of her castles even burned down."

"At least this is only one bad *day*," said Jessica, trying to cheer Judy up.

"*Day*-us horribilus!" Judy cried.

"We can still eat cookies," said Jessica. "And the tea will be iced tea."

Judy grabbed a crown-shaped cookie and dunked it in a cup of cold tea.

"Disgusting!" said Jessica. "Dunking food in tea is bad manners."

What did she expect when a person came from a long line of rotten rat catchers? Judy dunked her cookie again.

"I'm going down the street to check on something," said Jessica. "I'll be back in a flash."

Judy stared at the empty seats. This was not a right royal tea party. This was a *wrong* royal tea party. Because a party without friends was just plain no good. *Horribilus*.

❧   ❧   ❧

Stink burst into the tent with his smelly boy feet. Judy looked like she had a bad case of the Moody blues. She, Judy Moody, had boatloads of tea and no friends to drink it.

"Where is everybody?" Stink asked.

"My friends were no-shows," said Judy. "Nobody came. Not even you."

"Maybe they got the day wrong," said Stink.

"Saturday? I just reminded everybody yesterday."

"Maybe they got the time wrong," said Stink.

"Everybody knows high tea is at four p.m. sharp, Stink."

"Maybe they don't like tea," said Stink.

"Maybe they don't like *me*," said Judy. Even her swan napkin looked lonely.

"What's that noise?" They peered through the tent flap. Mum and Dad were blowing up ... a bouncy castle!

Judy and Stink zoomed across the yard. "Mum! Dad!" Judy called. "You said no bouncy castle!"

"It was Jessica's idea," said Dad.

"It's Mrs Soso's from down the street," said Mum.

"I knew she was getting one for her grandkid's birthday today," said Jessica. "She said we could use it for free if we return it."

Judy gazed at the castle. It had four towers with turrets and four flags flying. It was filled with balls. It even had an inflatable drawbridge slide.

"I need to borrow Stink for a minute," said Jessica, pulling him out front.

Judy crawled inside. She bounced.

Once. Twice. She stopped. Bouncy castles were absotively, posilutely no fun when you didn't have anybody to bounce with. *ROAR!*

She, Judy Moody, was in a royal blue mood. Why didn't she just listen to her friends in the first place? The tea party had been all about her – being a queen and getting a crown.

Pooh. If only she had it to do over, she wouldn't be such a Hooray Henrietta.

High Royal Tea Party

Judy heard a bell ringing. She peeked out of the bouncy castle. Stink was standing on the front sidewalk, ringing a bell. "Hear ye, hear ye!" shouted Stink.

"Her Royal Highness requests your presence at a royal tea party," said Jessica.

"Take a bounce in the bouncy castle," called Stink.

Rocky heard the bell from across the street at his house. Frank heard the bell on his way to Rocky's house. Amy saw the bouncy castle on her ride home from hip-hop class. In no time, Judy's friends were crowding into the bouncy castle.

Let the royal bouncing begin!

Rocky showed them how to do a flip and landed on his bum. Frank showed them how to pretend-fall and landed on his bum. Amy showed them crazy hip-hop dance moves. Jessica Finch bounced to third-grade spelling words. "S-E-C-R-E-T!"

When they were all bounced out, Judy announced, "Time for the right royal tea party ... and crowning!"

Everybody groaned.

"Tea sounds boring," said Frank.

"Sorry if I was a royal pain," said Judy.

"But I promise it will be smashing for everybody, not just me."

"Cross your heart and spit in a cat's eye?" asked Rocky.

"Cross my heart," said Judy. "But I'm not going to spit on Mouse."

Judy's friends trooped over to the T. P. tent. *Ta-da!* The tent winked and blinked and sparkled with twinkly lights. "Gold crowns for everyone!" said Judy. This time, her friends were going to get the royal treatment.

"Rocky, I crown you Royal Magician," said Judy.

"Awesome!" said Rocky. "My first magic trick is to make this royal cookie disappear!" *CHOMP.* He ate it!

"Frank, I crown you Royal Jester," said Judy. "You make everybody laugh."

"I love jokes. When is a piece of wood like a queen? *When it's a ruler!* What did the paste eater say to the queen? *Stick with me!*" Everybody cracked up.

Judy crowned Jessica Finch. "You are the Royal Secret Keeper." *Wink, wink.*

"Are we going to have a race?" asked Amy. "You said the queen loves pigeon races."

"No pigeons," said Judy. "But we can still have a race. I brought wind-up toys. Amy Namey, I crown you Royal Scribe. You can write about who wins the race."

"I accept, Your Ladyship," said Amy, bending to receive her crown.

"You forgot me," said Stink. "Don't give me a stinky job like Royal Bug Destroyer or Royal Rat Catcher or something."

"Or something." Judy let out a nervous laugh. "Stink, I crown you Royal Clock Keeper."

"Sounds easy."

"Not if you work for the queen and have to wind up one thousand clocks!" said Judy.

They played drop the hankie. They played guess what's in the queen's purse.

Jessica took out an old patent leather purse. "Pretend this is one of the queen's handbags. She has like three hundred of them. I played this game at Wolff Castle. I have a list of stuff that's really in the queen's purse. You guys have to try to guess what's in it."

"Mints!" said Amy. "The queen can't have bad breath."

"Crown jewels," said Rocky.

"Tennis racket!" yelled Stink.

"Tea bags," said Amy. "The queen can never be without tea."

"Hankies!" said Judy.

"A key to the Tower of London," said Frank.

"Mints and hankies are correct," said Jessica. She pulled out her list. "The queen also carries reading glasses, dog treats for her corgis, a crossword puzzle, a penknife and good-luck charms. Plus a lipstick and a mirror."

"Wow! No way! Cool!" everybody said.

"Guess what else. She uses her purse to send secret codes. Like if she puts her bag on the table, it means time to go in five minutes."

"Rare!" said Judy.

At last it was time for the race. Judy took out a shoebox full of wind-up toys.

"I'll take the chicken," said Amy. "It looks the most like a pigeon."

"I call the queen," said Jessica.

Judy wanted the queen, but she let Jessica have it. "I'll take the sock monkey that jumps rope."

"Hmm. I can't decide. Should I pick the wind-up eyeball or wind-up sushi?" Frank asked the others.

"Sushi!" said Stink and Rocky at the same time.

"Then I'll take the clacking teeth," said Rocky.

"I call the wind-up pants," said Stink.

Judy and Rocky put down tape for the starting and finish lines. "Time for the Frog Neck Lakeshire Grand National Wind-Up Toy Championship!" called Judy. "Where's our Royal Clock Keeper? Say when, Stink."

Everybody kneeled behind the starting line. They wound up their toys and held them in place. "Ready, set, GO!" yelled Stink.

"And they're off!" cried Amy.

"C'mon, Sushi!" yelled Frank.

"Go, Pants!" said Stink.

"You can do it, Queen Elizabeth!" yelled Jessica.

"Sock Monkey is in the lead," said Amy. "Oh, wait. He stopped to jump rope."

"The Queen and the Pants are neck and neck," cried Amy. "Chicken is close behind. The Clacking Teeth are taking a bite out of this race."

"Hurry up, Sushi!" Frank urged.

"Sushi and Chicken are now bringing up the rear. The Pair of Pants is giving the Queen a run for her money.

"Too bad! Sock Monkey is winding down.

"The Queen and Pants are still battling for the gold. Wait. We have a situation. The Pants are down!"

"No fair!" Stink set the pants upright again. "The Queen knocked Pants over with her handbag."

"Go, Queenie!" shouted Jessica.

"It's the Queen and Pants in the lead. The Queen is a step ahead. Looks like the Queen is... Wait. The Queen stopped to wave. Pair of Pants is in the lead. They're close to the finish. We have a winner and it's... Pair of Pants. The Pants win!"

"You did it, Pants!" yelled Stink. "We won! You're the best!"

After the race, everybody sipped tea and munched on yummy-scrummy crumb cakes.

Just then, Missy the dog walker came by with three dogs. One of the dogs was a corgi named Queenie. No lie. Everyone rushed over to pet her.

"I stopped by to give you a letter," Missy said. "It came to our house by mistake. Looks important."

A letter? "Thanks!" said Judy. "It must be from Tori."

"No problem," said Missy. "Say bye, Queenie."

Rocky looked over Judy's shoulder. "It's royal mail," said Rocky.

"With royal postage," said Frank.

"The postmark says Buckingham Palace. It's from the queen!" Jessica squealed.

"Cheese and crackers!" said Judy.

Frank put his crown on Judy's head. "We crown *you* Royal Letter Reader."

"Read it! Read it! Read it!" everybody chanted.

Dearest Judy Moody,

The Queen wishes me to thank you for your letter and kind message. The Queen was pleased to learn that you are making a family tree. Her Majesty took particular delight in your drawing of the Queen riding a hinny, which tickled her pink. The Queen has loved horses since her first riding lesson atop a pony at age three.

In answer to your questions 2 and 5, the Queen does find her crown quite heavy. It weighs 1.06 kg (2.3 pounds) – more than a bag of sugar!

Secondly, I can tell you the Queen prefers chocolate biscuits over eel pie (to avoid the royal burps), though, due to tradition, eel pie was served at her coronation.

Your thought for Her Majesty is greatly appreciated and I am to thank you, once again, for writing as you did.

Yours sincerely,

Jane Wigglebottom, The Queen's R.R.C.

R.R.C.! Royal Rat Catcher? The Queen's Royal Rat Catcher wrote her a letter?

"Look. It says R.R.C.," said Jessica.

Don't break the pinkie promise!

"It must be from the queen's Right Royal Correspondent," said Jessica.

Phew! It was the perfect end to a perfect party. It wasn't *horribilus* at all. "This T. P. is T. P." Judy announced. Her friends looked at her funny.

"This Tea Party is Total Pants."

Stink held his wind-up pants in the air. "Yeah it is! The Pants rule all!"

"I hate to tell you," said Jessica, "but *pants* is not a good thing. *Pants* means bad. Awful. Total nonsense. I think it also means *undies* in England."

"It does?" said Judy.

"It does?" said Stink.

"You really know your onions," said Judy.

"This party is total undies!" yelled Stink.

Tickety-boo. Judy Moody had held a right royal tea party after all. And it was spot-on smashing. The bee's knees. Fit for a queen!

Megan McDonald is the author of the popular Judy Moody and Stink series, as well as the Judy Moody and Friends series for new readers. She has written many other books for children, including the Ant and Honey Bee stories, the Sisters Club series and several picture books. Before she began writing full-time, Megan McDonald worked as a librarian, a bookseller and a living-history actress. She lives in Northern California with her husband, Richard Haynes, who is also a writer.

photo by Michele McDonald

Peter H. Reynolds is the illustrator of the popular Judy Moody and Stink series in addition to many other books, including several for which he is

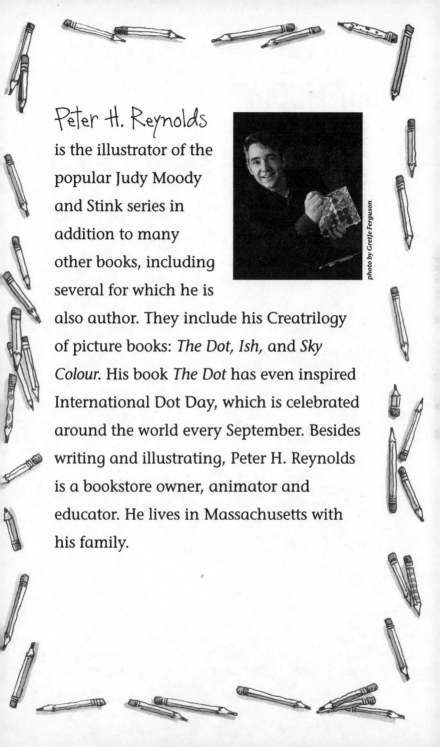

photo by Gretje Ferguson

also author. They include his Creatrilogy of picture books: *The Dot, Ish,* and *Sky Colour.* His book *The Dot* has even inspired International Dot Day, which is celebrated around the world every September. Besides writing and illustrating, Peter H. Reynolds is a bookstore owner, animator and educator. He lives in Massachusetts with his family.

IN THE MOOD FOR MORE JUDY MOODY? THEN TRY THESE!

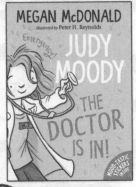

MEGAN McDONALD
Illustrated by Peter H. Reynolds
JUDY MOODY
Ciao!
AROUND THE WORLD IN 8½ DAYS

MEGAN McDONALD
Illustrated by Peter H. Reynolds
JUDY MOODY GOES TO COLLEGE
Genius!

MEGAN McDONALD
Illustrated by Peter H. Reynolds
JUDY MOODY GIRL DETECTIVE
Crumbs!

MEGAN McDONALD
Illustrated by Peter H. Reynolds
JUDY MOODY AND THE NOT BUMMER SUMMER
Thrill-a-delic!
BIG FOOT CLUB

MEGAN McDONALD
Illustrated by Peter H. Reynolds
JUDY MOODY AND THE BAD LUCK CHARM
Whoa!

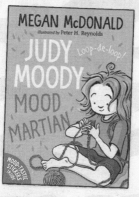

MEGAN McDONALD
Illustrated by Peter H. Reynolds
JUDY MOODY MOOD MARTIAN
Loop-de-loop!

MEGAN McDONALD
Illustrated by Peter H. Reynolds
JUDY MOODY AND THE BUCKET LIST
1-2-3, whee!

MEGAN McDONALD
Illustrated by Peter H. Reynolds
JUDY MOODY AND THE RIGHT ROYAL TEA PARTY

MEET JUDY MOODY'S BROTHER STINK!

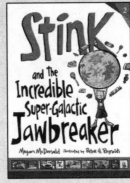
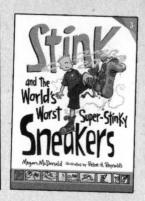

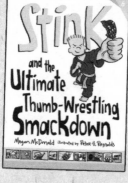

Stink and the Midnight Zombie Walk
Megan McDonald illustrated by Peter H. Reynolds

Stink and the Freaky Frog Freakout
Megan McDonald illustrated by Peter H. Reynolds

Stink and the Shark Sleepover
Megan McDonald illustrated by Peter H. Reynolds

Stink and the Attack of the Slime Mould
Megan McDonald illustrated by Peter H. Reynolds

Stink Hamlet and Cheese
Megan McDonald illustrated by Peter H. Reynolds

Stink-O-Pedia
SUPER STINKY STUFF FROM A to Z
Megan McDonald illustrated by Peter H. Reynolds

Stink-O-Pedia 2
MORE STINKY STUFF FROM A to Z
Megan McDonald illustrated by Peter H. Reynolds

JUDY MOODY AND STINK ARE STARRING TOGETHER!

In full colour!